THIS CANDLEWICK BOOK BELONGS TO:

_____

_____

_____

To Nathan and Naomi

D. K.

Text
copyright ©
2016 by
Dori Kleber
Illustrations copyright © 2016 by
G. Brian Karas

First paperback edition 2019

Library of Congress Catalog Card Number 2015934465

ISBN 978-0-7636-6819-8 (hardcover)
ISBN 978-1-5362-0971-6 (paperback)

20 21 22 23 24 CCP 10 9 8 7 6 5 4 3 2   Printed in Shenzhen, Guangdong, China

This book was typeset in Berlonia.   The illustrations were done in gouache and pencil on paper.

Candlewick Press   99 Dover Street   Somerville, Massachusetts 02144   visit us at www.candlewick.com

More-igami

illustrated by
G. Brian Karas

Dori Kleber

CANDLEWICK PRESS

Joey loved things that folded.

He collected old road maps.

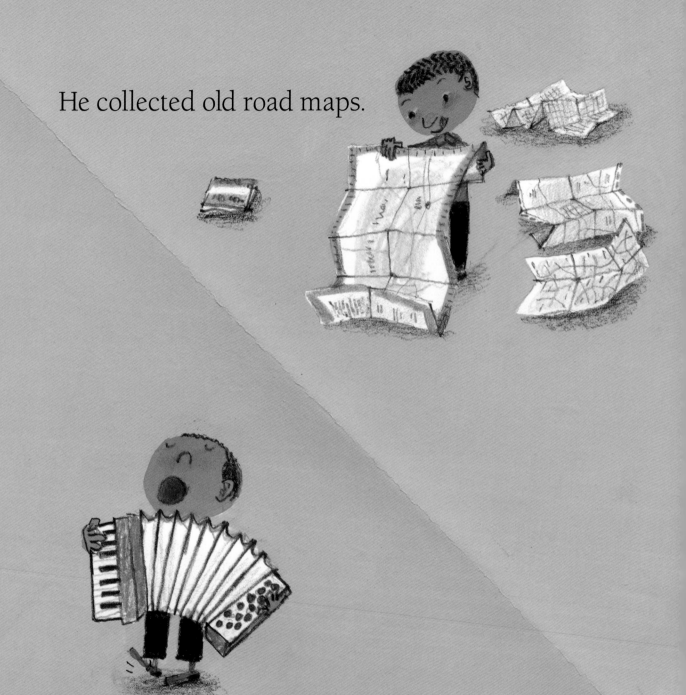

He played the accordion.

He slept in a foldaway bed.

One day, Sarah Takimoto's mother came to school.

She took a plain piece of paper.

She folded it,

and flipped it,

and pulled it,

until
it
became . . .

a crane.

Joey's eyes popped. His jaw dropped.
Mrs. Takimoto called it origami.

"I want to make origami," Joey told her.
"Will you teach me?"

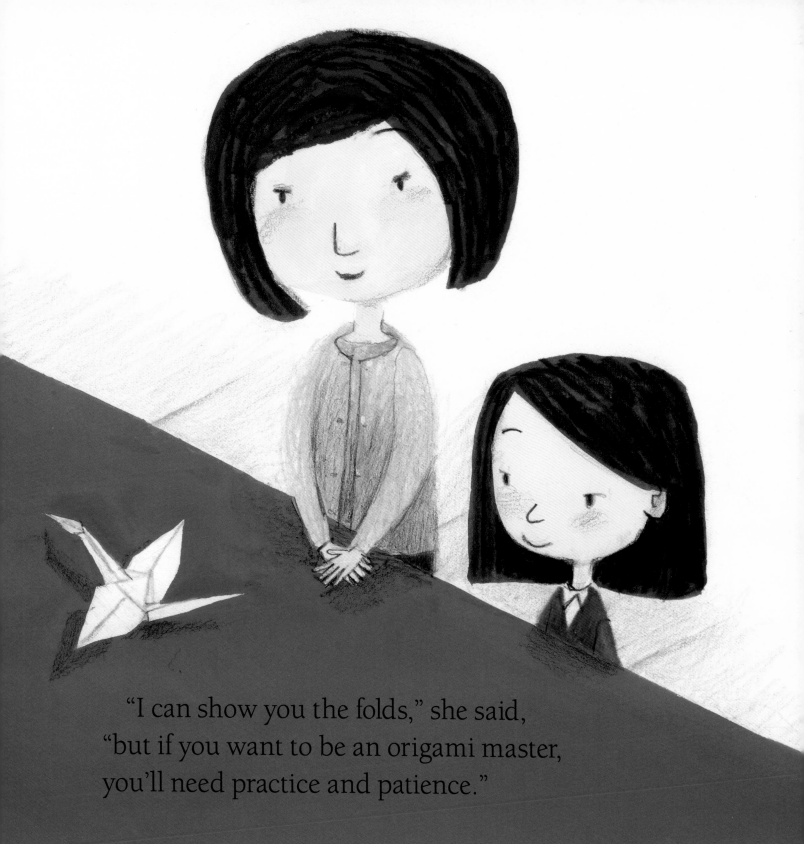

"I can show you the folds," she said,
"but if you want to be an origami master,
you'll need practice and patience."

Joey started that afternoon. He practiced on his notebook paper and on the construction paper from the art shelf. But even his simple shapes were crooked and crumpled.

So he practiced on his homework . . .

and on the newspaper . . .

and on his sister's
sheet music.

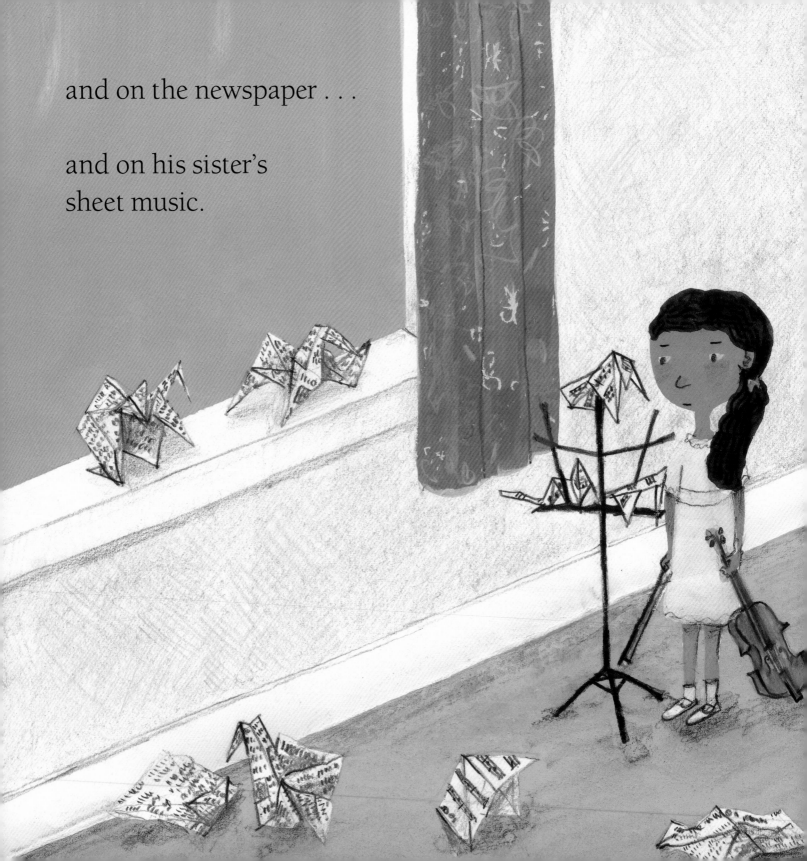

And he practiced on
all the gift wrap . . .

and on the recipe
for Aunt Vivian's
pineapple surprise . . .

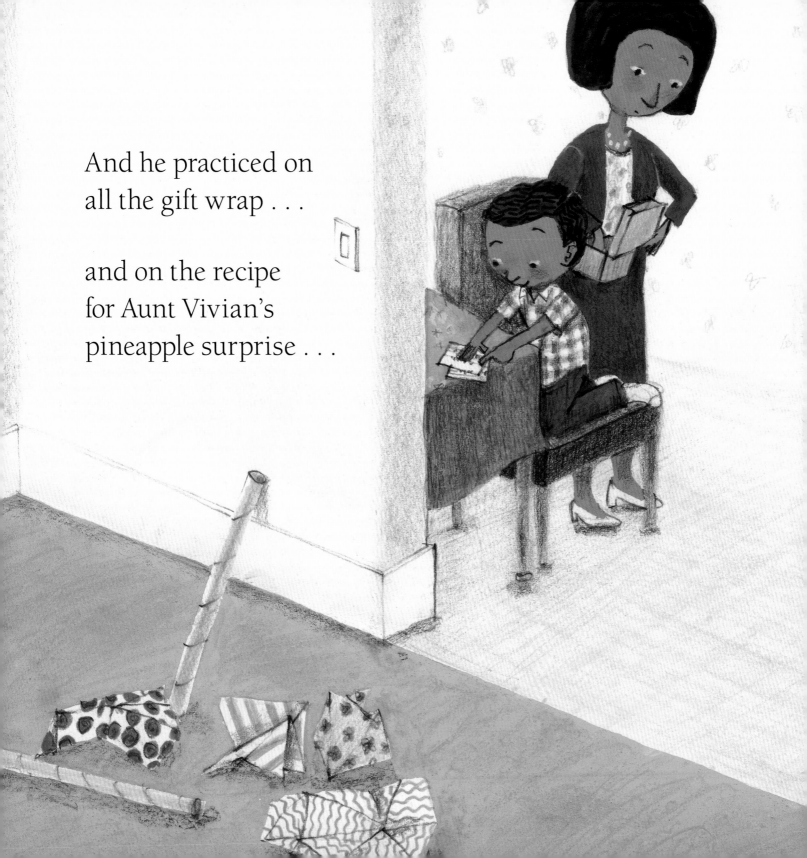

and on the thirty-eight dollars in Mom's purse.

"This folding has to stop," said Mom.

Joey drooped. How would
he ever become an origami
master without practice?

He went next door to Muy Mexicana.
Fajitas always made him feel better.

"Joey!" Mr. Lopez sang. "Hey, what's wrong?"

"It takes practice and patience to be an origami master," Joey said. "But whenever I practice, everybody else loses their patience."

"Many artists are misunderstood, *amigo*," said Mr. Lopez. "Especially when they are just learning."

"What's that?" Mr. Lopez asked, pointing to Joey's napkin.
"A pyramid," said Joey. "Sorry."
"No, don't apologize," Mr. Lopez said. "I like it.
It makes the table look fancy. Could you make more?"
Joey grinned. "I could make a hundred!"

So Joey folded and folded and folded until pyramids perched on every table in the restaurant.

Each day after school, Joey went back to Muy Mexicana. He folded napkins into fans.

He made candlesticks. Then he tried crowns.

Some napkins toppled. Others flopped. But Joey kept folding until they were perfect.

Finally, he was ready to try the most difficult fold of all.

He took a crisp napkin.

He folded.

He flipped.

He pulled.

It worked! A crane!

At last, he was an origami master.

Just then, a girl walked in. She was waving a paper fan.
Her eyes popped. Her jaw dropped.

"Did you make that?" she asked.
Joey nodded.

"I can show you how," said Joey. "But I should warn you. It takes practice—and lots of patience!"

Fold your own origami ladybug

Are you ready to make origami? Try this ladybug.

Keep practicing until it's just right!

1. Start with a square piece of paper. Fold it in half to make a triangle.

2. Fold the triangle in half. Press down hard to make a crease, then open it back up.

3. Now fold the top corners down so they reach a little past the bottom edge of the paper. Leave some space around the center crease.

4. Flip the paper over. Fold the top corner down to the center of your paper.

5. Then fold the point of that same corner back up, so it hangs over the top of the paper.

6. Flip the paper over again. Add some spots to the wings to make it look like a real ladybug.

You did it!

Dori Kleber was an award-winning journalist and business writer before she began writing children's books. *More-igami* is her picture-book debut. She lives just outside Atlanta.

G. Brian Karas has illustrated more than ninety children's books, including two books about Ant and Honey Bee by Megan McDonald, *Tap Tap Boom Boom* by Elizabeth Bluemle, *Night Job* by Karen Hesse, *Anywhere Farm* by Phyllis Root, and *Are You Going to Be Good?* by Cari Best, a *New York Times* Best Illustrated Children's Book of the Year. G. Brian Karas lives in the Hudson Valley of New York.